The CROW and the PITCHER

by Aesop
retold by Robert Newell
illustrated by Franklin Ayers

Scott Foresman

Editorial Offices: Glenview, Illinois • New York, New York
Sales Offices: Reading, Massachusetts • Duluth, Georgia
Glenview, Illinois • Carrollton, Texas • Menlo Park, California

Bear was so hot!
He wanted a drink.

Bear reached with both paws.
Too bad!
He could not quite reach it.

Mouse was so very hot!
She wanted a drink.

Mouse climbed.
Too bad!
Mouse could not quite climb it.

Crow was so very, very hot!
She wanted a drink too.

Too bad!
Crow almost fell in.

"Hmm," said Crow.
"Let me think about this."

Crow had an idea.
What did she decide?
She got some little rocks.

Splash!
In went a rock.

Splash! Splash!
In went two rocks

Splash! Splash!
Splash! Splash!
In went lots and lots of rocks.

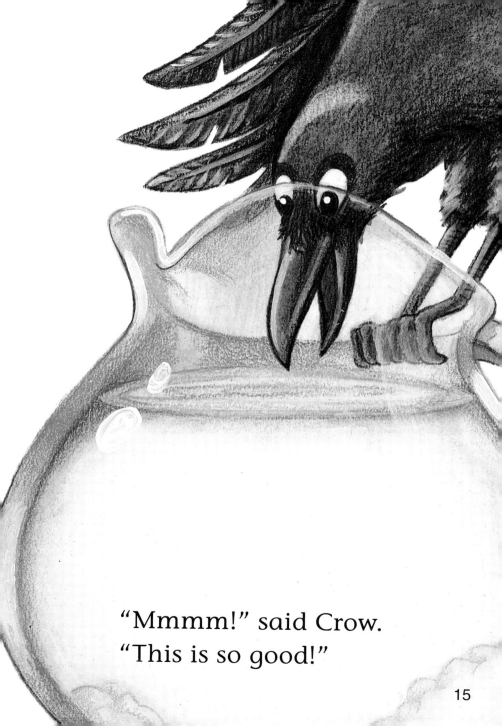

"Mmmm!" said Crow.
"This is so good!"

**Remember:
Do not give up.
Try!
Then try, try again.**